WITH LOVE TO
Gillian and Pearl

Sarah Garland
Billy and Belle

PUFFIN BOOKS

On Monday morning Billy lay
in bed for a long time.

He was thinking about his hamster,
and about the baby that would
soon be born.

He heard Dad filling the kettle.
He heard Mum dressing Belle.

He heard Spot barking.
He smelt toast burning.

He was late for breakfast.

Billy got ready for school.

Today, Belle was coming too

because Mum and Dad were
going to the hospital.

Billy and Belle were going to school with
Mrs Plum, the school secretary.

Belle was very excited.

Mrs Plum left them with the teacher.

Billy showed his friends his hamster.

Everyone had brought a pet.

John had a
tortoise.

Pat had a
rat.

Rita had a
frog.

Donna had a
guinea pig.

Hassan had a
caterpillar.

Kelly had a
mouse.

Dino had a
beetle.

Sam had a
snail.

Alan had a
gerbil.

Anna had a
rabbit.

Billy had a
hamster.

And Belle had
a spider.

The teacher looked at the spider,

then she put the pets out in the playground.

She asked the class to draw their pets.

Belle tried to remember how
many legs her spider had,
but she couldn't . . . so . . .

she went quietly outside

to look for her spider.

She looked and looked . . .

and looked, until at last

she found it

on her jumper.

At playtime . . . what a shock . . .

...he pets had escaped!

It took the children a long time to find them.

When they had settled down again,

Billy showed them his picture.

Three o'clock. Pet day was over.

Dad told Billy and Belle the news.

They talked about the baby,

and ate their tea,

and got ready for bed.

Billy lay in bed,
thinking about the baby.

He heard a cab stop outside.
He heard Dad running up the stairs.

Billy and Belle saw
their new brother for the first time.

And Billy's hamster woke up.